KNOCK KNOCK DINOSAUR

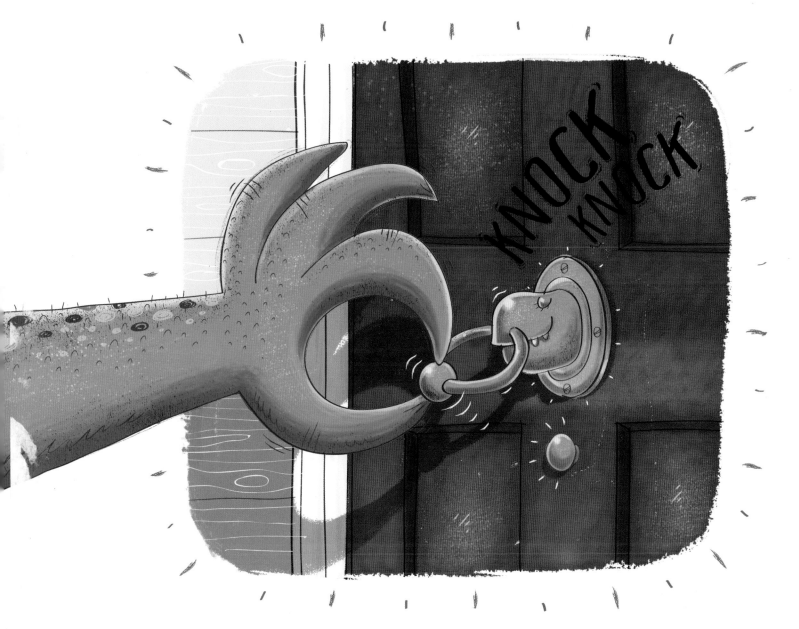

KNOCK KNOCK

Caryl Hart and Nick East

For Andrew x C.H.
For Ruby, Daisy and Lola x N.E.

HODDER CHILDREN'S BOOKS

First published in Great Britain in 2017 by Hodder and Stoughton

Text © Caryl Hart 2017
Illustrations © Nick East 2017

The moral rights of the author and illustrator have been asserted.

A CIP catalogue record of this book
is available from the British Library.

HB ISBN: 978 1 444 92847 1
PB ISBN: 978 1 444 92849 5

10 9 8 7 6 5 4 3 2 1

Printed and bound in China.

FSC
www.fsc.org

MIX
Paper from
responsible sources
FSC® C104740

Hodder Children's Books
An imprint of
Hachette Children's Group
Part of Hodder and Stoughton
Carmelite House
50 Victoria Embankment
London EC4Y 0DZ

An Hachette UK Company
www.hachette.co.uk

www.hachettechildrens.co.uk

Hodder
Children's
Books

KNOCK KNOCK
DINOSAUR

Caryl Hart and Nick East

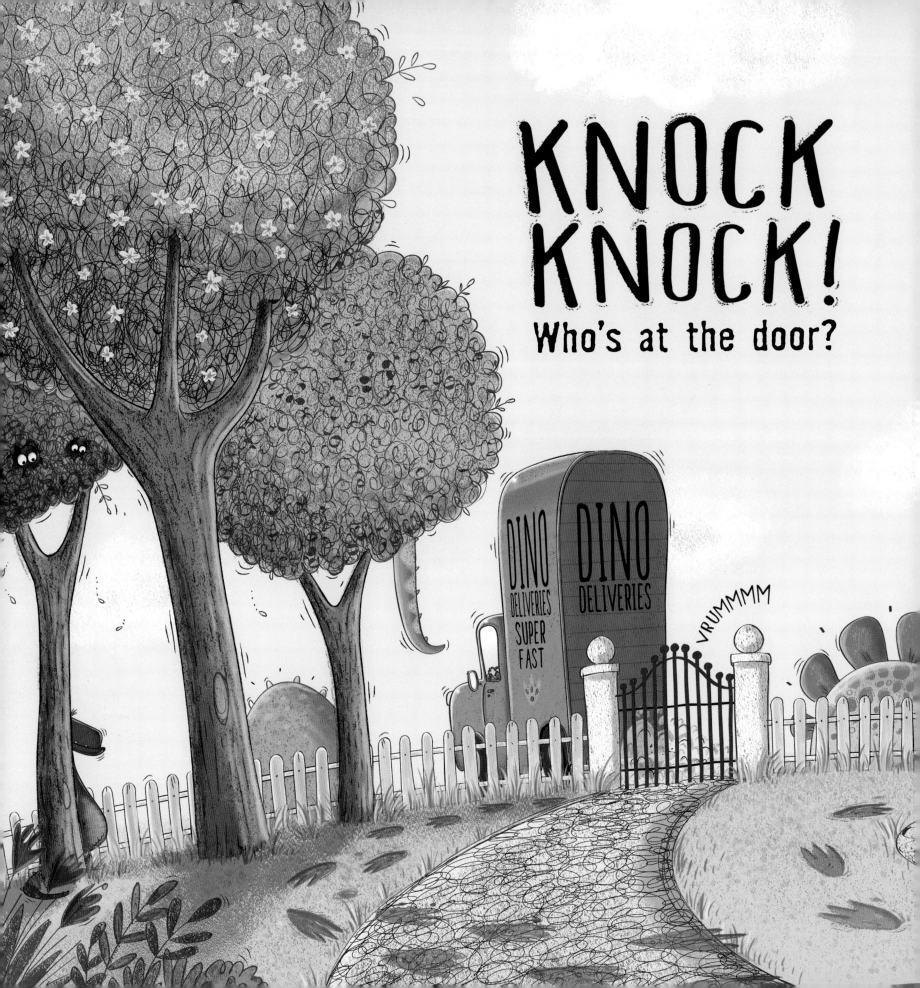

SNORT

DELIVERY

Woah! ONE real live dinosaur!
He smiles at me. He waves his claw.

I say "Hi," and he says...

ROARRR

"My mum's in town," I try to say.
"We weren't expecting guests today."
But the T-rex sniffs and rubs his tummy.
He thinks Mum's apple pie smells yummy.

I say, "Perhaps you'd like some lunch?"
He thunders past then...

MUNCH
CRUNCH
CRUNCH!

"This is kind of fun," I think
as I pour the dinosaur a drink.

But something makes a dreadful crash.
It's TWO triceratops,

THUMP BUMP BASH!

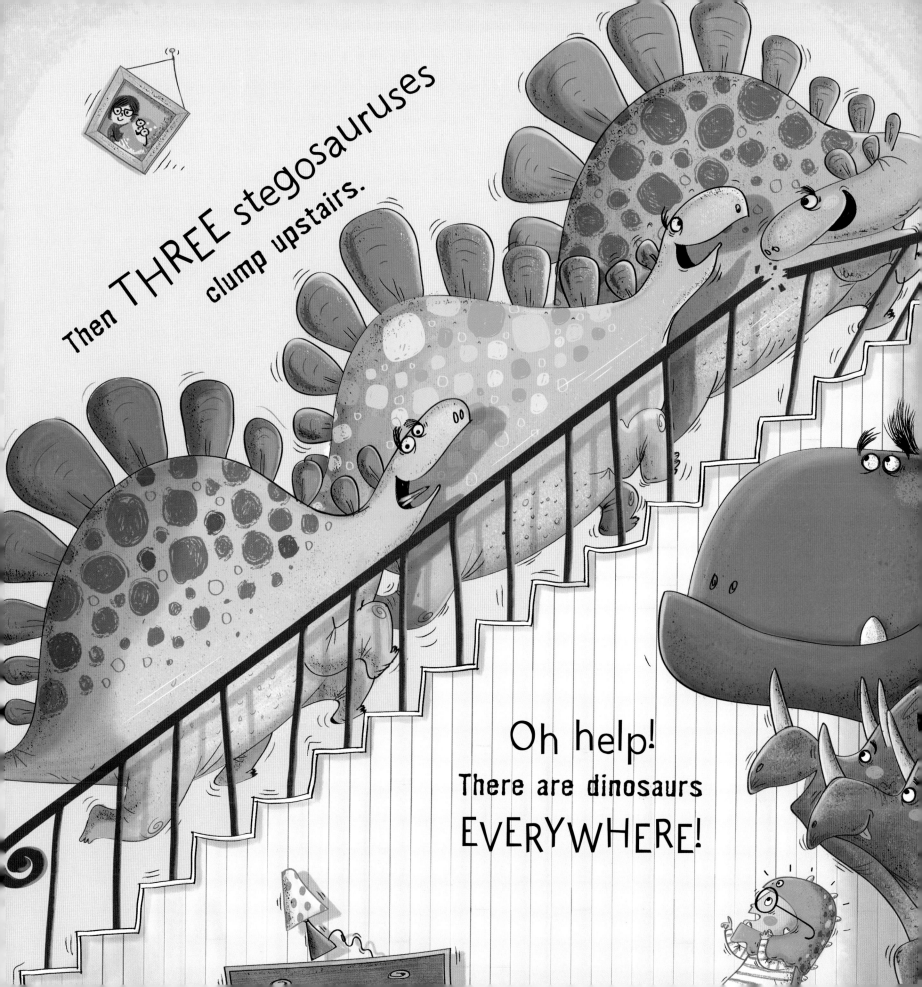

Then THREE stegosauruses clump upstairs.

Oh help!
There are dinosaurs
EVERYWHERE!

This is not good! What shall I do?
They're coming through the windows
and down the chimney too.

FOUR velociraptors are drawing on the wall.

FIVE allosauruses skateboard down the hall.
The kitchen's in chaos, the dining room's a mess,
and who's in the garden is anybody's guess!

From upstairs comes a bubbly laugh.
There are SIX apatosauruses
splashing in the bath!

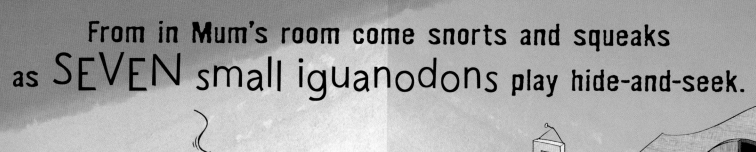

From in Mum's room come snorts and squeaks
as SEVEN small iguanodons play hide-and-seek.

"Oh goodness, this has gone too far —
someone's wearing Mum's new bra!"

EIGHT giganotosauruses
have knickers on their heads.
And NINE oviraptors
are jumping on the beds.
"Hey!" I yell. "You can't do that!"
TEN pterodactyls play 'Catch Dad's Hat'.

BOING
BOING

HEY!

The bath goes SPLOSH!

The mirrors SMASH!

The bed springs GROAN!

A vase goes CRASH!

"That's it!" I say. "You've had your fun.
It's time to go — now off you run!"
But the dinosaurs beg — "Oh, let us stay!
We're having such a lovely play!"

I stamp my foot,
I grab the mop.
Then shout out...

"EVERYBODY STOP!"

SCREECH

The T-rex shrugs. "You PAID for us,
so what's the point of all this fuss?
Just read this note, you'll see we're right.
It says so here in black and white."

I read the note. I rub my eyes.
"Dinosaur play set ACTUAL SIZE!"

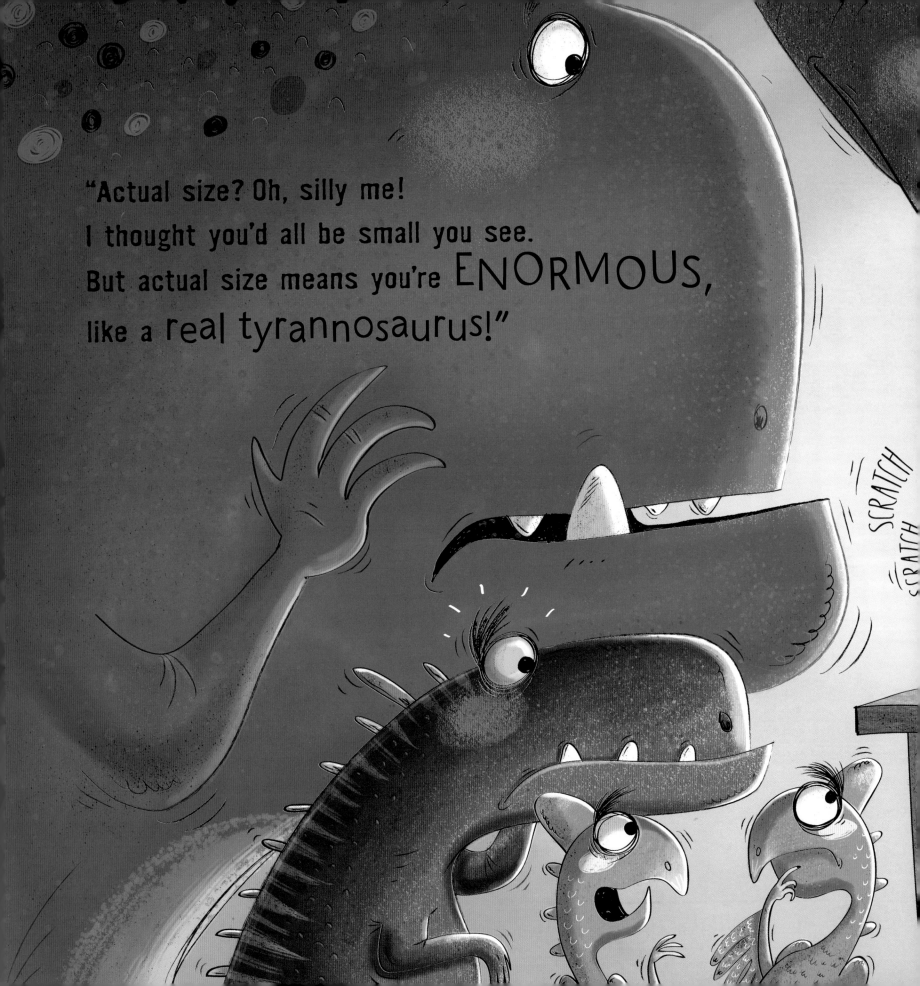

"Actual size? Oh, silly me!
I thought you'd all be small you see.
But actual size means you're ENORMOUS,
like a real tyrannosaurus!"

SCRATCH
SCRATCH

It seems Mum made a small mistake,
an error ANYONE could make.
She didn't read the small print right
when she clicked ORDER late last night.

Just then I hear a car arrive.
Its tyres are crunching up the drive.

"Mum's home!" I cry. "Now we're in trouble.
Just look at all this dust and rubble!

She won't be happy, not at all,
to see those claw marks on the wall!"

"Don't worry," say the dinosaurs.
"We're used to doing household chores."
Then round and round the house they rush

SWISH SWISH

So when Mum walks in through the door,
the house is cleaner than before!

She puts her heavy shopping down.
"What's happened while I've been in town?"

"Not much," I say,
"I stayed indoors...

...playing with my dinosaurs."